A Note to Parents

For many children, learning math[...] math!" is their first response — to wh[...] add "Me, too!" Children often see adults comfortably reading and writing, but they rarely have such models for mathematics. And math fear can be catching!

The easy-to-read stories in this **Hello Math** series were written to give children a positive introduction to mathematics and parents a pleasurable re-acquaintance with a subject that is important to everyone's life. **Hello Math** stories make mathematical ideas accessible, interesting, and fun for children. The activities and suggestions at the end of each book provide parents with a hands-on approach to help children develop mathematical interest and confidence.

Enjoy the mathematics!
• Give your child a chance to retell the story. The more familiar children are with the story, the more they will understand its mathematical concepts.
• Use the colorful illustrations to help children "hear and see" the math at work in the story.
• Treat the math activities as games to be played for fun. Follow your child's lead. Spend time on those activities that engage your child's interest and curiosity.
• Activities, especially ones using physical materials, help make abstract mathematical ideas concrete.

Learning is a messy process and learning about math calls for children to become immersed in lively experiences that help them make sense of mathematical concepts and symbols.

Although learning about numbers is basic to math, other ideas, such as identifying shapes and patterns, measuring, collecting and interpreting data, reasoning logically, and thinking about chance are also important. By reading these stories and having fun with the activities, you'll help your child enthusiastically say "**Hello, Math**," instead of "I hate math."

—Marilyn Burns
National Mathematics Educator
Author of *The I Hate Mathematics! Book*

For the kids in Room 5
—C.H.

For Gerry
— B.D.

Copyright © 1995 by Scholastic Inc.
The activities on pages 35-40 copyright © 1995 by Marilyn Burns.
All rights reserved. Published by Scholastic Inc.
HELLO READER!, CARTWHEEL BOOKS, and the CARTWHEEL BOOKS logo are registered trademarks of Scholastic Inc.

Library of Congress Cataloging-in-Publication Data

Holtzman, Caren.
    A quarter from the tooth fairy / by Caren Holtzman ; illustrated by Betsy Day.
        p.   cm.—(Hello math reader. Level 3)
    "Cartwheel Books."
    Summary: A boy has trouble deciding how to spend the quarter he gets from the Tooth Fairy.
    ISBN 0-590-26598-9
    [1. Tooth Fairy—Fiction. 2. Stories in rhyme.]   I. Day, Betsy, ill.   II. Title.   III. Series.
PZ7.H7425Qu   1995
[E]—dc20   95-13232
                                                        CIP
                                                        AC

12 11 10 9 8 7 6 5 4 3 2 1   5 6 7 8 9/9 0/0

Printed in the U.S.A.   23

First Scholastic printing, October 1995

A Quarter
from the
Tooth Fairy

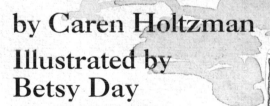

by Caren Holtzman

Illustrated by
Betsy Day

Hello Math Reader — Level 3

SCHOLASTIC INC.
Cartwheel BOOKS ®
New York   Toronto   London   Auckland   Sydney

I found a shiny quarter
where I put my tooth last night.
I could hardly wait to spend it.
But I wanted to do it right.

I jumped up on my bicycle
with the money from the fairy.
I knew just what to do with it —
buy a monster from my friend, Mary.

I hadn't had that monster long,
when I was surprised to find,
it didn't feel right. It felt all wrong.
I guess I changed my mind.

I raced over to Mary's house,
and made it just in time.
Mary took her monster back.
I got a nickel and two dimes.

I rode my bike around the block
and came to my favorite store.
I parked my bike and, cash in hand,
I walked right through the door.

I saw gum balls, kites, and
games, games, games.
Too sticky. Too big. Too much.
So I bought a spaceship pencil.
It was the perfect touch.

I hadn't had that pencil long,
when I was surprised to find,
it didn't feel right. It felt all wrong.
I guess I changed my mind.

I turned and rode back to the store,
the pencil in my sack.
I gave the clerk the pencil
and I got five nickels back.

I had the change in my pocket
when I saw my old friend, Jim.
Jim said, "It's hot, but I know what!
Come with me. We'll swim."

I still had my money with me when
we finally reached the pool.
And there I bought Lupe's blue goggles
because they looked so cool.

I hadn't had those goggles long
when I was surprised to find,
they didn't feel right. They felt all wrong.
I guess I changed my mind.

When Jim and I found Lupe,
she was flipping over at Kenny's.
She was happy to have her goggles back
in exchange for 25 pennies.

Now that I had my money back,
I thought about what to do.
I stopped to look at the animals
and bought a sticker at the zoo.

I hadn't had that sticker long
when I was surprised to find,
it didn't feel right. It felt all wrong.
You guessed it! I changed my mind.

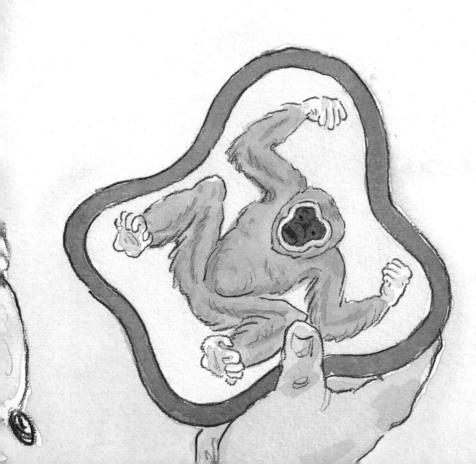

The woman at the zoo was nice.
She said, "Here's your quarter, kid."
By now I was pretty tired from
all the buying and returning I did.

It seemed so very silly
to keep changing and changing my mind.
Suddenly I had a great idea.
This was an idea of a whole new kind.

I hurried on home to my house
and, yes, I am telling the truth.
The quarter went under my pillow
and I bought back my tooth!

• ABOUT THE ACTIVITIES •

Learning about money is abstract and complicated for young children for several reasons: Having more coins does not necessarily mean having more money; larger coins aren't always worth more than smaller ones; and the names of coins have no logical connection to their value (there's nothing in the names *quarter*, *dime*, *nickel*, or *penny* that give children clues about how much a coin is worth).

The activities and games in this section give children firsthand experiences that help them learn about money. The directions are written for you to read along with your child. You'll need a collection of coins — at least 3 quarters, 3 dimes, 6 nickels, and 25 pennies. You'll also need a small paper lunch bag.

Children may enjoy doing their favorite activities again and again. Encourage them to do so. Or try a different activity at each reading. Be open to your child's interests, and have fun with math!

—Marilyn Burns

You'll find tips and suggestions
for guiding the activities whenever
you see a box like this!

Retelling the Story

The boy in the story changed his mind over and over again. Each time, he returned what he had bought and got back different coins.

Check in the story to see what the boy was given. Take out the same coins he got each time. Then count up the money to check that the boy got 25 cents.

Making Sense Out of Cents

Take real coins and look at them carefully. What pictures, words, and numbers do you notice? Can you find where the penny says, "ONE CENT"? Where the nickel says "FIVE CENTS"? That tells how much each coin is worth.

You're on your own with the dime and quarter. The dime says "ONE DIME" on the back instead of "TEN CENTS." And the quarter says "QUARTER DOLLAR" on the back, but not "TWENTY-FIVE CENTS." You'll just have to remember.

A money tip: The shortcut for writing "cents" is ¢. It's the letter "c" with a line through it. Try writing it!

Grab Bag Games

One at a Time

Put three pennies, three nickels, three dimes, and three quarters into your bag. Now reach in and try to pick out a penny. Feel around until you think you have one. No peeking! Check your coin. If you got another by mistake, put it back and try again.

Play again, but try to get a nickel. Then do the same for a dime and a quarter.

Two at a Time

Now try picking out two coins. First try two nickels. Then try one nickel and one dime.

If your child is interested, keep going!
Name coins for your child to find. Let your child call out coins for you to pick. Ask your child to decide if you pulled the correct coins.

Exactly Right

Ready for a harder game? Use the same bag of coins. Reach in. Try to take out coins so you have exactly 12¢. (Remember ¢ means "cents.") Spread out your coins to figure how much you have. If you haven't got 12¢, just try again! Try other amounts, too.

Write down amounts for your child to find or have your child write amounts for you to pick. Writing gives practice connecting the mathematical symbols to the coins.

More Games with Coins

Older or Younger?

Take a penny from the bag. Look at the year it was made. Who is older—you or the penny? Figure this out for other coins in the bag.

How Many Ways?

This is a hard game, *really* hard. Find all the different ways to make change for a quarter. There are 12 different ways altogether. Three ways are shown in the story. Can you figure out the rest? Here's a hint: To keep track, make piles of coins or write down the coins you use.

To build all 12 possibilities, you'll need to have $3.00 in coins—8 dimes, 22 nickels, and 110 pennies. It's a chunk of change, but there's no substitute for hands-on learning!